Prawns at Dawn

INTRO TO PHASE 5

/aw/

Level 4+
Blue+

Helpful Hints for Reading at Home

The graphemes (written letters) and phonemes (units of sound) used throughout this series are aligned with Letters and Sounds. This offers a consistent approach to learning whether reading at home or in the classroom.

THIS BLUE+ BOOK BAND SERVES AS AN INTRODUCTION TO PHASE 5. EACH BOOK IN THIS BAND USES ALL PHONEMES LEARNED UP TO PHASE 4, WHILE INTRODUCING ONE PHASE 5 PHONEME. HERE IS A LIST OF PHONEMES FOR THIS PHASE, WITH THE NEW PHASE 5 PHONEME. AN EXAMPLE OF THE PRONUNCIATION CAN BE FOUND IN BRACKETS.

Phase 3			
j (jug)	v (van)	w (wet)	x (fox)
y (yellow)	z (zoo)	zz (buzz)	qu (quick)
ch (chip)	sh (shop)	th (thin/then)	ng (ring)
ai (rain)	ee (feet)	igh (night)	oa (boat)
oo (boot/look)	ar (farm)	or (for)	ur (hurt)
ow (cow)	oi (coin)	ear (dear)	air (fair)
ure (sure)	er (corner)		

New Phase 5 Phoneme	aw (draw, claws, dawn)

HERE ARE SOME WORDS WHICH YOUR CHILD MAY FIND TRICKY.

Phase 4 Tricky Words			
said	were	have	there
like	little	so	one
do	when	some	out
ome	what		

TOP TIPS FOR HELPING YOUR CHILD TO READ:

• Allow children time to break down unfamiliar words into units of sound and then encourage children to string these sounds together to create the word.

• Encourage your child to point out any focus phonics when they are used.

• Read through the book more than once to grow confidence.

• Ask simple questions about the text to assess understanding.

• Encourage children to use illustrations as prompts.

RO TO
SE 5

:w/

This book introduces the phoneme /aw/ and is a Blue+ Level 4+ book band.

Prawns at Dawn

Written by
William Anthony

Illustrated by
Kris Jones

The red fish you can see there is Erika.

The fish you can see with the drawing pen is Keeth. Erika and Keeth are not pals.

Keeth and Erika get into brawls a lot.
You see, they like pranks.

The best thing Keeth did was draw on Erika when she slept.

To get back at him, Erika hid some crabs in Keeth's bed.

A crab can pinch with its claws. And Keeth can tell you that the claws hurt.

But Keeth did a prank so big that Erika said they must do prawns at dawn.

Keeth cut her lawn. But what did Keeth cut into her lawn?

Yes, that is right. Keeth cut a big bum into her lawn!

That night, Erika said, "We have to do prawns at dawn!"

But what is prawns at dawn? Well, six prawns are laid down at dawn.

One fish gulps, then the next fish gulps, and they go on and on.

But one prawn is bad! The fish that gets it must swim far and never come back.

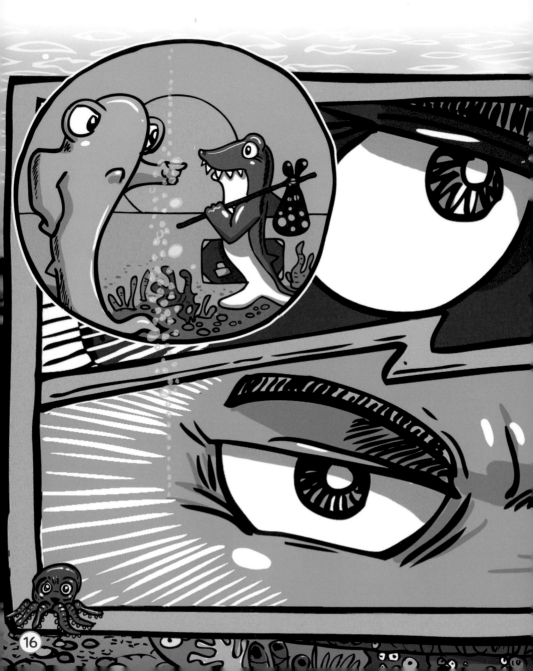

16

The next morning, Keeth and Erika sat down for prawns at dawn.

Prawns at dawn was there to sort things for good. They agreed.

"So, it has all come down to this," said Keeth.

"I am afraid it has," said Erika. "Now, we pick a prawn."

"I cannot look," said one of the fish.
"3... 2... 1..."

"Yuck!" said Erika and Keeth.
"A pair of bad prawns?" said Keeth.

"There must be just one bad prawn in prawns at dawn!" said Erika.

"Yes," said a fish from the crowd.
"But we are fed up with the pranks!"

"So we laid down six bad prawns," said the fish.

"Now the pair of you must swim far and never come back!" said a fish at the back.

"Unless... you agree to stop the pranks and get along," said a little fish.

Erika and Keeth did not wish to swim far and never come back. They shook fins.

From then on, they never did a prank.
It was the end of prawns at dawn.

Prawns at Dawn

1) Can you explain how prawns at dawn is played?

2) Why did Erika demand to play prawns at dawn with Keeth?

3) How many bad prawns ended up on the table?
   a) One
   b) Three
   c) Six

4) Do you think Erika and Keeth can put aside their differences and live peacefully?

5) Have you ever had to put aside your differences with someone? How did it make you feel?

©2022 **BookLife Publishing Ltd.**
King's Lynn, Norfolk PE30 4LS

ISBN 978-1-80155-053-6

Prawns at Dawn
Written by William Anthony
Illustrated by Kris Jones

An Introduction to BookLife Readers...

Our Readers have been specifically created in line with the London Institute of Education's approach to book banding and are phonetically decodable and ordered to support each phase of the Letters and Sounds document.

Each book has been created to provide the best possible reading and learning experience. Our aim is to share our love of books with children, providing both emerging readers and prolific page-turners with beautiful books that are guaranteed to provoke interest and learning, regardless of ability.

BOOK BAND GRADED using the Institute of Education's approach to levelling.

PHONETICALLY DECODABLE supporting each phase of Letters and Sounds.

EXERCISES AND QUESTIONS to offer reinforcement and to ascertain comprehension.

BEAUTIFULLY ILLUSTRATED to inspire and provoke engagement, providing a variety of styles for the reader to enjoy whilst reading through the series.

AUTHOR INSIGHT:
WILLIAM ANTHONY

William Anthony's involvement with children's education is quite extensive. He has written over 60 titles with BookLife Publishing so far, across a wide range of subjects. William graduated from Cardiff University with a 1st Class BA (Hons) in Journalism, Media and Culture, creating an app and a TV series, among other things, during his time there.

William Anthony has also produced work for the Prince's Trust, a charity created by HRH The Prince of Wales, that helps young people with their professional future. He has created animated videos for a children's education company that works closely with the charity.

INTRO TO PHASE 5

/aw/

This book introduces the phoneme /aw/ and is a Blue+ Level 4+ book band.